ABOUT THE BANK STREET READY-TO-READ SERIES

More than seventy-five years of educational research, innovative teaching, and quality publishing have earned The Bank Street College of Education its reputation as America's most trusted name in early childhood education.

Because no two children are exactly alike in their development, the Bank Street Ready-to-Read series is written on three levels to accommodate the individual stages of reading readiness of children ages three through eight.

○ *Level 1:* **GETTING READY TO READ (Pre-K–Grade 1)**
Level 1 books are perfect for reading aloud with children who are getting ready to read or just starting to read words or phrases. These books feature large type, repetition, and simple sentences.

● *Level 2:* **READING TOGETHER (Grades 1–3)**
These books have slightly smaller type and longer sentences. They are ideal for children beginning to read by themselves who may need help.

○ *Level 3:* **I CAN READ IT MYSELF (Grades 2–3)**
These stories are just right for children who can read independently. They offer more complex and challenging stories and sentences.

All three levels of The Bank Street Ready-to-Read books make it easy to select the books most appropriate for your child's development and enable him or her to grow with the series step by step. The levels purposely overlap to reinforce skills and further encourage reading.

We feel that making reading fun is the single most important thing anyone can do to help children become good readers. We hope you will become part of Bank Street's long tradition of learning through sharing.

The Bank Street College of Education

For Bill Hooks
—E.S.

For Rosemary
—G.C.

THE BOY WHO CRIED "WOLF!"
A Bantam Book/February 1994

*Published by Bantam Doubleday Dell Books
for Young Readers, a division of Bantam
Doubleday Dell Publishing Group, Inc.
1540 Broadway, New York, New York 10036.*

*Special thanks to James A. Levine, Betsy Gould,
Rosemary Sandberg, and Matt Hickey.*

Library of Congress Cataloging-in-Publication Data

Schecter, Ellen.
The boy who cried "Wolf!" / retold in rebus by Ellen Schecter:
illustrated by Gary Chalk.
p.   cm.—(Bank Street ready-to-read)
"A Byron Preiss book."
Summary: Uses rebuses to retell
the Aesop fable about a young boy
whose false cries for help
bring him to an unfortunate end.
ISBN 0-553-09043-7. — ISBN 0-553-37232-7
1. Rebuses. [1. Fables.   2. Rebuses.]   I. Chalk, Gary, ill.
II. Title   III. Series
PZ8.2.S34Bo   1994
398.21—dc20
[E]
92-37202   CIP   AC

Published simultaneously in the United States and Canada

PRINTED IN THE UNITED STATES OF AMERICA

0 9 8 7

Bank Street Ready-to-Read™

The Boy Who Cried "Wolf!"

Retold in rebus
by Ellen Schecter
Illustrated by Gary Chalk

A Byron Preiss Book

A BANTAM BOOK
NEW YORK • TORONTO • LONDON • SYDNEY • AUCKLAND

Long ago,

when the world was still wild,

there was a young boy.

He earned his living

taking care of sheep.

Every day, as the ⬤ sun rose,

the 🎩 boy led the 🐑 sheep

from the 🏠 village.

He took them to

a big, green ☁ meadow

where the 🌱 grass

grew sweet and thick.

"Be sure to call for HELP
if a wolf comes,"
his master told him.
"All the people in
the village will run
to help you."

All day,

as the ⬤ sun shone bright,

the 🧑 boy played his 🪈 flute

and kept watch

over the 🐑 sheep.

For nearby there was
a deep, dark forest
full of hungry wolves.
Silently and swiftly
the wolves crept
among the trees.

They watched the ⬛ sheep
with hungry eyes.

For maybe you know that
a 🐺 wolf likes nothing better
than a delicious dinner of
tender 🍖 lamb chops!

One very hot day,

the boy grew tired

watching the sheep

in the bright sun.

It was so quiet

he could almost hear

the grass grow.

To stay awake, the boy
pretended he saw wolves
in the clouds.
He imagined the wolves
creeping like shadows
into the grassy meadow.

Then the boy

had a wicked idea.

He jumped up and ran

toward the 🏠 village.

"HELP!" he cried.

"A 🐺 wolf is eating

the 🐑 sheep!"

The boy's shouts rang
through the village.
"HELP! Wolf!"
all the people cried.
They ran to the meadow
as fast as they could.

But all they found
was the boy
laughing so hard he could
hardly stand.
The sheep were
safe and sound,
munching the sweet, thick grass.

"But where is the wolf?"
cried the people.
"There is no wolf,"
laughed the boy.
"It was just a joke.
I wanted to see if you
would come."

All the people
were very angry
as they turned back
toward the village.

"Don't ever do that again!"
scolded the master.
"I won't," promised the boy.
But he kept on laughing
and laughing.

A few days later,
the boy grew tired
of playing his flute
and watching the clouds.
He could barely keep
his eyes open.

Then he remembered what fun

he had watching

all the people

run from the village

to help chase away the wolf!

The boy jumped up
and ran to the village.
"HELP! Wolf!" he cried.
Once again all the people
ran to help.

But again there was no wolf.
The sheep were munching
the fresh, green grass.
And once again the boy
just laughed and laughed.

All the people
mumbled and grumbled.
"Don't expect us to come again,"
they told the boy.
His master frowned.
"How can I ever trust you again?"

But the boy
was laughing so hard
he couldn't hear a word.

Then one evening,

as the red sun

set in the sky,

the boy fell fast asleep.

Shadows crept out of

the deep, dark forest.

And a real wolf
crept out with them!
Suddenly the wolf
jumped from the shadows
and attacked the sheep.

The boy awoke and ran

to the village.

"HELP! Wolf!" he shouted.

 People heard him.

But they did not believe him.

"There is no wolf," they said.

"HELP! Wolf!"
the boy cried again.

"How many times does
that boy think
he can fool us?"
 people asked.

The people were tired
after working all day.
Some were eating their supper.
Others were rocking their babies.

"You won't catch us running
to help that liar!" they said.
Even the boy's master
just yawned
and soaked his tired feet.

"HELP! Wolf!"
the boy cried once more.
All the people heard him.
But this time no one believed him.
This time no one ran to help.

The wolf
killed many sheep
before it slipped back
into the forest.
And all the people
ever found of the boy
was his little flute.

So maybe now you see
why no one believes a liar...
even when he tells the truth.